This book belongs to

_____

MAMA'S AFRO IS A SOLDIER TOO

Mom's Cancer Diagnosis Explained

Written by N.M. Charles
Illustrated by Mary K. Biswas

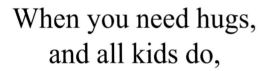

When you need hugs,
and all kids do,

Whether you feel happy,
afraid, or blue,

There's an amazing person
who always comforts you.

1

Her name is Mama, and you know it's true.
But did you know Mama's afro is
a soldier too?

2

Mama is strong and brave and loves you so.

She works hard and fights every day just to see
you grow.

One day, cancer started growing in her body.
A group of very naughty cells that can cause some worry.
It is trying to hurt Mama though you cannot see it.

But Mama is a soldier and will not back down one bit.
Just you wait and see, cancer doesn't have a clue that
Mama's afro is a soldier too.

In the battles she faces, Mama will go through changes.
The doctors will help her in the fights she engages.

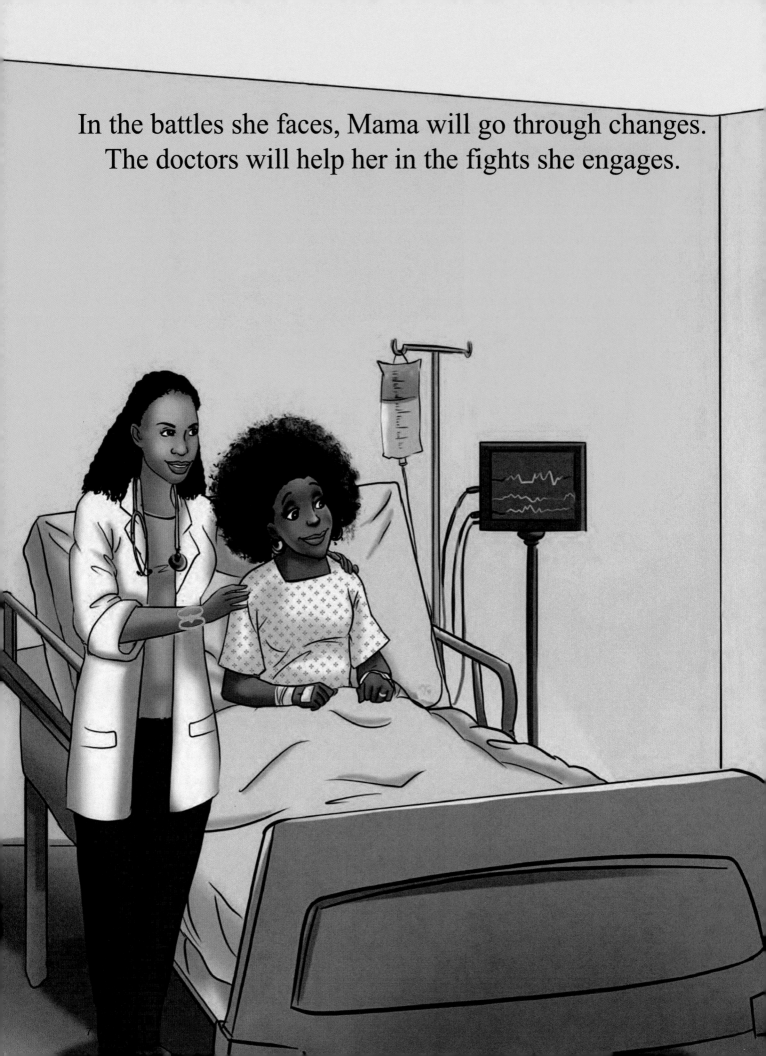

She will have some scars and at times be a little sore,
but just remember, Mama's a soldier to her core.

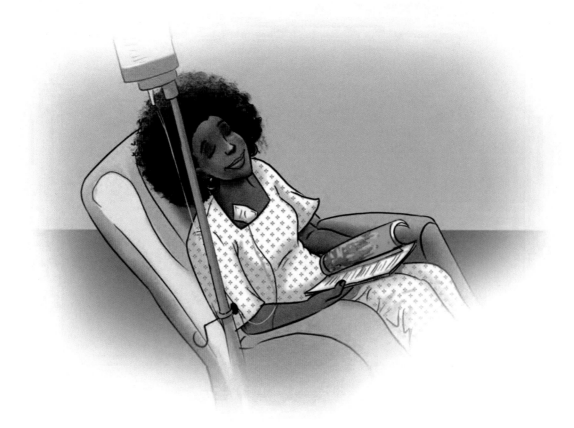

She may have to do chemo,
which is a mix of helpful drugs.

It may make her tired, so be sure to
give her lots of gentle hugs.

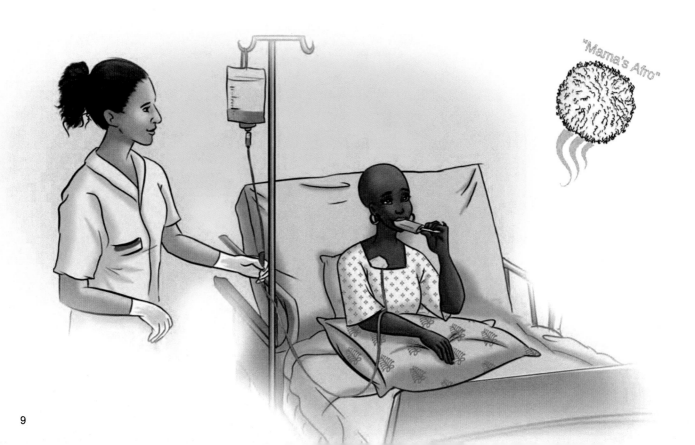

"Mama's Afro"

Her hair may go away as hairs with chemo sometimes do,
But then Mama's afro BECAME a soldier too.

Mama's afro hair has always been fierce, strong, and curly.

It has always been a part of her and her personal history.

With the chemo medicine, her beautiful afro has joined the fight, against the naughty cancer cells with all its mighty might.

12

So when you see Mama's smooth, bald head, there is
no cause for alarm, because her friend,
the Afro Soldier is just working her charm.

Mama may look different
but is still a queen.

Only now her power and
strength are easier seen.

Afro Soldier has another friend in this fight.
Its name is Radiation, a very special light.

It comes from a big machine in which Mama lays,
and it helps to get rid of the naughty cancer cells
over several days.

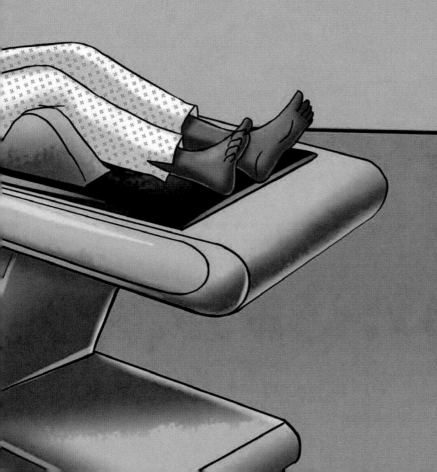

So keep showing Mama all your love.
She welcomes kisses and smiles from her little turtle doves.

17

And just remember, to fight this battle, Mama is doing all that she can do, along with her afro...a great soldier too. 18

Commentary from Dr. Lisa Newman

A new diagnosis of cancer generates many emotions: fear for life and survival; confusion regarding the physical and psychological effects of cancer treatment; and anger at intrusion of the disease into one's life, with its financial toll and the disruption of personal as well as professional activities. For a parent, all of these emotions are eclipsed by anxiety regarding how to protect the children from the complex effects of the cancer experience.

Children deserve honesty from their parents, and a cancer diagnosis often results in difficult conversations. Using cancer of the breast as an example, most breast cancers occur in women. This usually means that mom must explain surgery and/or medical treatments that will change her appearance. Children also need reassurance from parents that everything possible will be done in order to take care of the disease successfully.

For the children of African American breast cancer patients, all of these complicated emotions and conversations feature unique perspectives. African American women tend to be diagnosed with breast cancer at relatively younger ages, when it is more likely that children are still in the household; socioeconomic disadvantages are more prevalent in African American families, which increases the financial strain of completing treatment; and African Americans are disproportionately under-represented in the healthcare workforce, which can magnify the tensions created by facing treatments in the foreign environment of a cancer center.

N.M.'s book cannot change the epidemiology of cancer nor can it create health equity. However, it indeed fills the huge void that had previously existed with regard to African American cancer patients having a resource that meets their special needs as parents. This book can be shared by parent and child together, providing comfort, encouragement and even humor during an otherwise traumatic journey. N.M.'s powerful message to both: you are not alone!

Dr. Lisa Newman, MD MPH FACS FASCO,is
the Chief, Section of Breast Surgery
Weill Cornell Medicine (WCM)Cancer Center
Chief, Breast Cancer Disease Management Team,
Chief of the Breast Surgical Oncology Programs -
the New York Presbyterian-Weill Cornell Medicine Network
Department of Surgery.

Commentary from Author N.M. Charles

When I was diagnosed with breast cancer, my daughters were just 5 and 3 years old. They were my first thoughts when I got the news. I wanted to be honest with them. I had to make them understand what to expect over the next year of treatment which could have included some physical changes such as loss of hair, skin changes, extreme fatigue, etc. Above all, I needed to help them not be afraid. It was new territory for me and I had to do things right. I decided to use a children's book to explain what Mama had to go through. Because they were so young, it was important to me that they related to the mom character in the book, not just as a fictional character but as one who looked like and whom they could recognize...as me.

At the time, that book did not exist for me. So I decided to write a book for future Mamas who would also have that need for their children to recognize them in the literature. However, any mom can use this book.

The book explains the various cancer treatment stages as a mom goes through the 'seasons' of surgery, chemotherapy and radiation. Additionally, through the Afro Soldier, a symbol of dual significance is provided. On one level, it symbolizes the fighting spirit of moms going through cancer, that inner drive and determination of not giving up whether it is through researching treatment options or enduring physical discomfort while ensuring normalcy for our children. On another level, it gives young readers a visual symbol of reassurance and hope. Even though mom is going through changes due to her illness, children do not have to be alarmed because they can trust that a strong little soldier is fighting to help her get better.

'Change' is also a subtle background character in the book which is depicted by the change in seasons from summer to autumn. My journey coincidentally started in the same summer to autumn seasons and progressed through those seasons and beyond.

Much of the background story and illustrations in the book mirror my own family life. I take my kids to the waterpark every summer, they play the violin, I give piggyback rides to both of my kids simultaneously (well back then I did), I worked on class projects and costumes during my treatment. Even the bunk bed I finally got for them, much to their excitement was eventually only 'half used' as they returned to sleep together on the bottom bunk.

Mama's Afro Is A Soldier Too deliberately does not specify a particular type of cancer. Why? Because moms all over the world are affected by a number of different cancers. The book can be used by any family whose mom is undergoing any kind of cancer treatment. I want to thank all the people who were there for me during the most challenging period of my life - the medical staff at New York Presbyterian/Weill Cornell hospital and Memorial Sloan Kettering (doctors, nurses, nurse practitioners, the phlebotomists, the administrative staff, etc.), my old friends, my new friends and of course my 2 little turtle doves who were the reasons I fought as hard as I did.

A percentage of my book sales will be donated to the New York City Chapter of Sisters Network Inc. - a national organization dedicated to raising awareness of breast cancer in the African American community.

To my daughters Jojo and Ellie
who lovingly kissed my shiny bald chemo head.
I love you now, I will love you tomorrow and
I will love you always and forever...

-N.M. (Mama)

ARIEL AND ROSE

Library of congress control number: 2020915520
Text copyright and illustrations copyright © 2021 by N.M. Charles.
Edited by: Christina Kover, Suzanne Brahim, Lisa and Damian Brewster, Bozena "Bibi" Budzynska.
Special thank you to all my beta readers.
Designed by N.M. Charles.
Published by Ariel & Rose Publishing Company. 1636 3rd Ave, Suite 108. New York, NY. 10128.
www.arielandrose.com
Ariel & Rose and the distinctive Ariel & Rose logo are registered trademarks of
Ariel & Rose Publishing Company. Printed in USA and China. For information, permissions or
special discounts for bulk purchases, please contact info@arielandrose.com.

Publisher's Cataloging-In-Publication Data
(Prepared by The Donohue Group, Inc.)

Names: Charles, N. M., author. | Biswas, Mary K., illustrator.
Title: Mama's afro is a soldier too : Mom's cancer diagnosis explained /
    written by N.M. Charles ; illustrated by Mary K. Biswas.
Description: First edition. | New York, NY : Ariel & Rose Publishing
    Company, 2021. | Interest age level: 003-009. | Summary: "Mom's
    strength, bravery, and cancer diagnosis are explained through a fierce
    little character—'The Afro Soldier.'"--Provided by publisher.
Identifiers: ISBN 9781735134109 (hardcover) | ISBN 9781735134116 (ebook)
            ISBN 9781735134123 (paperback)
Subjects: LCSH: Cancer--Diagnosis--Juvenile fiction. | African Americans--
    Health and hygiene--Juvenile fiction. | African Americans--Family
    relationships--Juvenile fiction. | Courage--Juvenile fiction. |
    Hairdressing of African Americans--Juvenile fiction. | CYAC: Cancer--
    Fiction. | African Americans--Health and hygiene--Fiction. | African
    Americans--Family relationships--Fiction. | Courage--Fiction. |
    Hairdressing of African Americans--Fiction.
Classification: LCC PZ7.1.C4913 Ma 2021 (print) | LCC PZ7.1.C4913 (ebook)
    | DDC [E]--dc23

RESOURCES

Listed below, are organizations that provide information and support to children whose families have been affected by cancer.

National (US) Cancer Support Services

American Cancer Society

"Helping children when a family member has cancer"
Phone +1-800-227-2345
https://www.cancer.org/treatment/children-and-cancer/when-a-family-member-has-cancer.html
Provides a series of guides offering extensive information on helping children understand and deal with cancer in another family member.

Cancer Support Community

"What do I tell the Kids?"
Phone +1-888-793-9355
https://www.cancersupportcommunity.org/sites/default/files/d7/document/
what_do_i_tell_the_kids.pdf
Booklet providing ways to talk to children of different ages about a family member's cancer.

CancerCare

"Helping children and teens understand when a parent or loved one has cancer"
Phone +1-800-813-HOPE(4673)
https://www.cancercare.org/connect_workshops/9-cancer_parent_or_loved_one_2011-04-20
Recorded teleconference with specialists giving tools to help children and teens cope.

CancerCare for Kids

https://www.cancercare.org/forkids
Provides support to children and adolescents affected by cancer. Services are free of charge and provided by professional oncology social workers who specialize in working with children and adolescents.

National Cancer Institute

"Talking to children about your cancer"
Phone +1-800-422-6237
https://www.cancer.gov/about-cancer/coping/adjusting-to-cancer/talk-to-children
Information to help you talk to your kids, teens, and adult children about cancer.

International Resources

Canadian Cancer Society

"Parenting when you have cancer"
Phone +1-416-961-7223
https://www.cancer.ca/en/cancer-information/living-with-cancer/your-relationships-and-cancer/
parenting-when-you-have-cancer/?region=on
Provides recommendations and strategies that can be used with children at home.

Macmillan Cancer Support, United Kingdom (UK)

"Talking to children and teenagers when an adult has cancer"
Phone +44 (0) 808-808-0000
https://cdn.macmillan.org.uk/dfsmedia/1a6f23537f7f4519bb0cf14c45b2a629/803-source/talking-to-children-and-teenagers-when-an-adult-has-cancer
Provides tips and a booklet to help you through the conversation with children, e.g. who should tell them; choosing the right place and time; how to tell them; and important points to tell them.

COLORING PAGE

Pick flowers for Mom

Put books on the shelf

Clean up your toys

Draw a picture for Mom

COLORING PAGE

Ages 5 to 6

Give water to pets

Clean up spills

Sort the laundry by color

Bring Mom a glass of water

Coloring Page

Ages 7 to 9

Help Mom put groceries away

Set the table

Spend time gardening together

Make a simple snack for Mom

COLORING PAGE

All ages

Make a memory box with Mom

Ask questions if confused

Allow Mom to rest

Tell Mom a joke

FIND THE SYMBOL CHALLENGE

There are 5 Adinkra symbols hidden in 10 locations throughout the book. Can you find them? In the spaces below, write the page number(s) and location where the symbols appear.

'Okodee Mmowere'
Strength

Page Number:

Location:

Page Number:

Location:

'Aya'
Endurance

Page Number:

Location:

Page Number:

Location:

'Kwatakye Atiko'
Bravery

Page Number:

Location:

Page Number:

Location:

'Akofena'
Courage

Page Number:

Location:

Page Number:

Location:

'Nyame Biribi Wo Soro'
Hope

Page Number:

Location:

Page Number:

Location:

ANSWERS: **Strength** Pg 6 Medical Center Window, Pg 9 Pillow; **Endurance** Pg 11 Cloud, Pg 15 Radiation Machine; **Bravery** Pg 3 Mama's Sleeve, Pg 11 Sidewalk; **Courage** Pg 10 Bed Footboard, Pg 13 Mama's Red Dress; **Hope** Pg 7 Doctor's Bracelet, Pg 18 Tree Carving.

A Journaling Guide

"Journaling is an outlet tool. It helps kids process and express their feelings and thoughts on paper so that they can make sense of troubling or confusing situations. Young children are impacted by what they see, what they experience and any changes in their routine. Here are some useful prompts* to help your child(ren) journal during this time."

-N.M.

Write or draw how you feel:

- o at the end of this story
- o if Mom loses her hair
- o if Mom needs to rest
- o if Mom cannot attend an event e.g. school play, soccer

- o when Mom goes to the doctor
- o when the whole family dances together
- o when you and Mom create a memory book together
- o when you play in the sprinklers in the summer

What things can you do to feel better when you are [insert emotion] e.g. sad/angry/worried etc.?

Write or draw about a funny experience with your family or friends.

Name or draw 3 things you can do to help Mom at home. How do you feel when you help Mom?

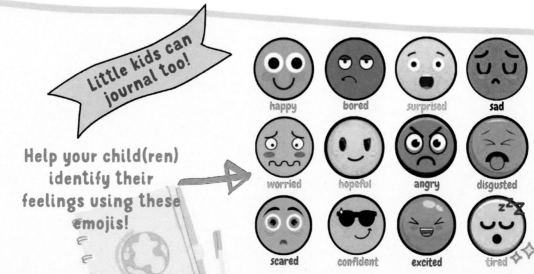

Little kids can journal too!

Help your child(ren) identify their feelings using these emojis!

happy   bored   surprised   sad
worried   hopeful   angry   disgusted
scared   confident   excited   tired

*Children's reactions to difficult news depend on their age, stage of development, personality and a number of other factors. These prompts are just a few ideas. However, it is best to take your child's lead on how <u>they</u> feel and what <u>they</u> want to write or draw in their journal pages.

YOUR JOURNAL

Write or draw a picture of your feelings, thoughts, hopes and experiences.

Name: _____   Date: _____

Draw a picture:

Write or draw whatever feels right.

See Printables Tab on www.arielandrose.com for additional blank pages.

29

Your Journal

Write or draw a picture of your feelings, thoughts, hopes and experiences.

Name: _____ Date: _____

Draw a picture:

Write or draw whatever feels right.

See Printables Tab on www.arielandrose.com for additional blank pages.

30

YOUR JOURNAL

Write or draw a picture of your feelings, thoughts, hopes and experiences.

Name: _____   Date: _____

Draw a picture:

Write or draw whatever feels right.

See Printables Tab on www.arielandrose.com for additional blank pages.

YOUR JOURNAL

Write or draw a picture of your feelings, thoughts, hopes and experiences.

Name: _____   Date: _____

Draw a picture:

Write or draw whatever feels right.

See Printables Tab on www.arielandrose.com for additional blank pages.

32

Adinkra Symbols, Names & Meanings

Adinkra are visual symbols from West Africa that are used to represent ideas, expressions, concepts, principles, values, traditional wisdom or thoughts. They were originally created by the Ashanti of Ghana and the Gyaman of Cote d'Ivoire (Ivory Coast) in West Africa.

	'Okodee Mmowere'	Strength
	'Aya'	Endurance
	'Kwatakye Atiko'	Bravery
	'Akofena'	Courage
	'Nyame Biribi Wo Soro'	Hope

Made in the USA
Middletown, DE
24 September 2021